Pumpkin Pumpkin

by Jeanne Titherington

A MULBERRY PAPERBACK BOOK

New York

WITH SPECIAL THANKS TO SAM

COLORED PENCILS WERE USED FOR THE FULL-
COLOR ART. THE TEXT TYPE IS ITC CASLON NO. 224
AND THE DISPLAY TYPE IS CASLON OPEN FACE.

LIBRARY OF CONGRESS CATALOGING IN PUBLICATION DATA

TITHERINGTON, JEANNE.
PUMPKIN PUMPKIN.
SUMMARY: JAMIE PLANTS A PUMPKIN SEED AND,
AFTER WATCHING IT GROW, CARVES IT, AND SAVES
SOME SEEDS TO PLANT IN THE SPRING.
1. CHILDREN'S STORIES, AMERICAN.
[1. PUMPKIN——FICTION.
2. GARDENING——FICTION] I. TITLE.
PZ7.T53PU 1985   [E]   84-25334
ISBN 0-688-09930-0

FOR

JAMES AND THE FISH

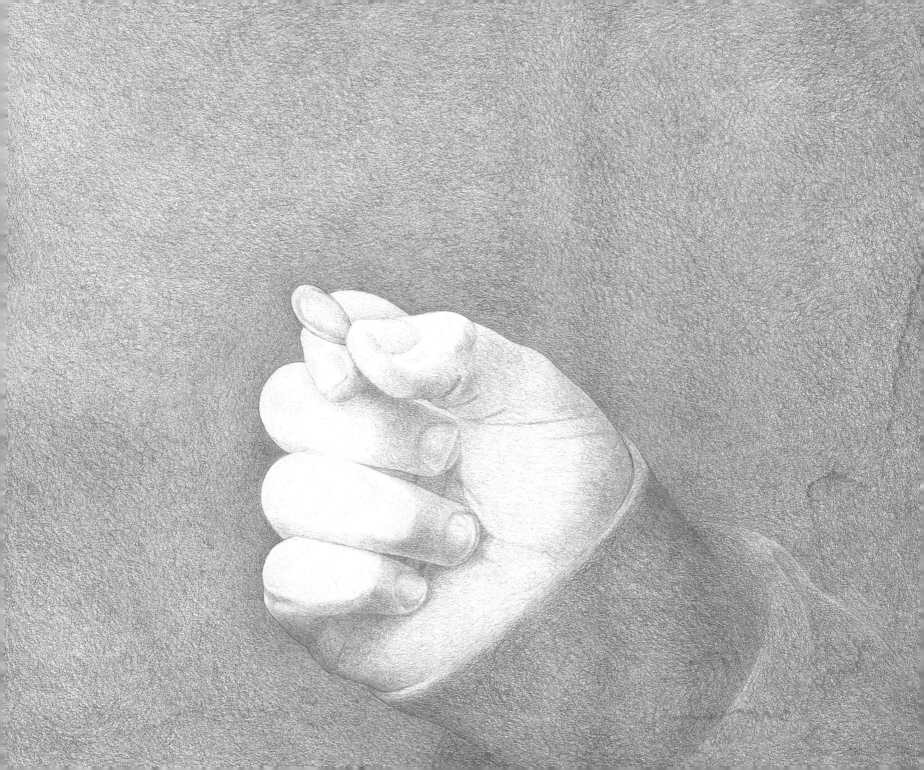

Jamie planted
a pumpkin seed,

and the pumpkin seed
grew a pumpkin sprout,

and the pumpkin sprout
grew a pumpkin plant,

and the pumpkin plant
grew a pumpkin flower,

and the pumpkin flower
grew a pumpkin.

And the pumpkin grew…

and grew…

and grew,

until Jamie picked it.

Then Jamie scooped out
the pumpkin pulp,
carved a pumpkin face,
and put it in the window.
But…

he saved
six pumpkin seeds
for planting in the spring.